Best Loved Bedtime

Stories

The Folktales
Illustrated by Tony Wolf
Written by Peter Holeinone
Adapted from works by Hans Christian Andersen,
Charles Perrault, The Brothers Grimm,
Giambattista Basile, and Alexander Afanasjev

The Stories of Robinson and Tom and Penny
Illustrated by Tony Wolf
Written by Peter Holeinone

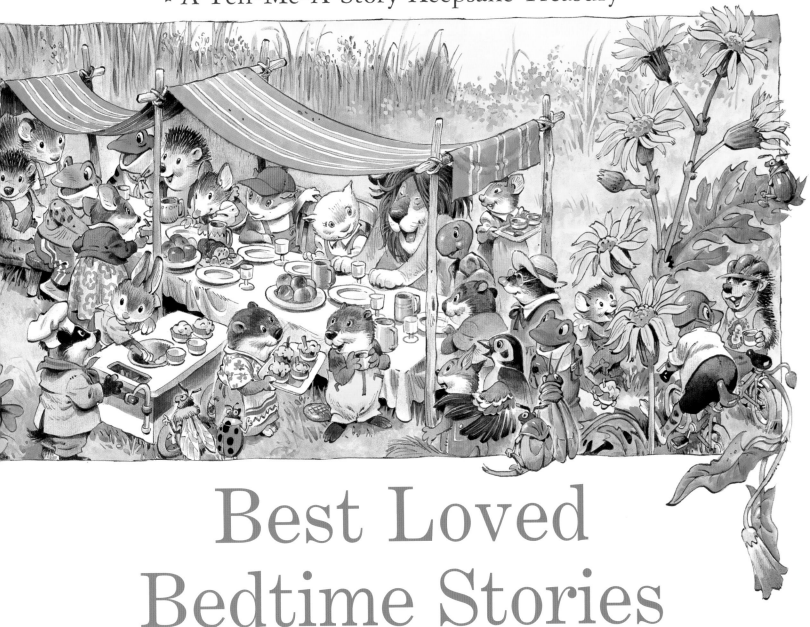

★ A Tell-Me-A-Story Keepsake Treasury ★

Best Loved Bedtime Stories

Dalmatian Press

BEST LOVED BEDTIME STORIES
Copyright © 2004 Dami International, Milano

All rights reserved
Printed in China

Editor: Louise Gikow
Cover Design: Emily Robertson

Published in 2004 by Dalmatian Press, LLC.
The DALMATIAN PRESS name and logo are trademarks
of Dalmatian Press, LLC, Franklin, Tennessee 37067.
No part of this book may be reproduced or copied in any form
without the written permission of Dalmatian Press.

ISBN: 1-40370-771-5
13314-0604

05 06 07 SFO 10 9 8 7 6 5 4 3 2

Tell Me A Story.

When you read a story to your child, lots of good things happen. You show your child that reading is exciting and fun. You encourage the growth and development not just of your little one's imagination but also his or her vocabulary, comprehension skills, and overall school readiness.

Research shows, time and time again, that children who are read to on a regular basis do significantly better in school than children who are not read to at home. We encourage you to spend ten to twenty minutes every day reading to your child. It's a small amount of quality time that reaps a big reward!

It's also important to keep reading books *to* your child and *with* your child even after he or she is reading independently. You can share books that are slightly more difficult than what your child is reading on his or her own because you are available to help with vocabulary words and any questions your child may have about the story.

Read and Discuss.

No matter how old your child is, or how well she is reading independently, remember that story time is the perfect opportunity to talk about what you're reading and any other topics that might arise from it. This kind of dialog helps make stories come alive and adds depth to your child's reading experience.

What would you do if you were in the story? you might ask. *How might you fix this problem? Did the character do the right thing?* and so forth.

Your child's Keepsake Treasury includes dialogic questions throughout the stories to prompt meaningful and memorable conversations. Ask your own questions as well. You might be surprised at the imaginative discussions that follow. You can learn more about dialogic reading online at: *http://www.readingrockets.org.*

We hope that *Best Loved Bedtime Stories* will become a treasured part of your family's library.

Happy Reading!

CONTENTS

THE UGLY DUCKLING

Once upon a time, down on an old farm, a mother duck sat on her seven eggs.

One nice morning, the eggs hatched. One by one, six little ducklings popped out.

They were yellow and fuzzy and totally adorable. Mother Duck loved them at first sight.

But the seventh egg didn't hatch. It was bigger than the others, and Mother Duck couldn't remember laying it. How had it gotten there?

But before Mother Duck could wonder any more, she heard a pecking from inside the shell... and the seventh egg finally hatched.

But what was this? A strange-looking duckling with grayish feathers who was bigger than the rest was standing there, looking at her.

"What an ugly duckling he is!" Mother Duck thought to herself. "How could that duckling be one of mine?"

Mother Duck was a good mother, however, so she kept her thoughts to herself. And she raised the ugly duckling as one of her own.

He learned to swim and dive and quack just like his brothers and sisters. The only thing he didn't do was eat like them! In fact, he ate much more, and he grew bigger and bigger.

Day after day, the ugly duckling's life grew more difficult.
Not only was he big, but he was awkward as well.

Soon, his brothers and sisters wouldn't play with him.

"You are too clumsy!" they said. "You ruin all our games.
Go away, you ugly duckling!"

This made him very sad.

Things were no better in the barnyard, either.

The rooster, the pig, and all the other ducks all laughed at
him. "What an ugly duckling," they said.

Mother Duck tried to protect him. "Poor little ugly duckling,"
she would say. "Why are you so different from all the others?
Where did you come from?"

Sadly, this made him feel even worse.

So he decided to run away.

One morning, just as the sun had come up, he left the barnyard and set out for the wide, wide world.

Everywhere he went, he asked the birds he met the same question.

"Do you know any ducklings who look like me?"

He asked the little bluebirds in the meadow. But they said no.

He asked the mallards in a nearby pond. But they said no.

He asked some geese in a swamp down the river. But they said no.

They also warned him to stay clear of the men with the guns.

"You will never find other ducklings like yourself if the men get you," they told him.

The ugly little duckling was beginning to believe that he should have stayed home. Even though everyone made fun of him, at least he was safe with Mother Duck!

One day, the ugly duckling found himself near an old woman's cottage. The old woman couldn't see very well. Thinking that he was a goose, she caught him and put him in a cage.

"I'll fatten her up," the old woman thought. "And then she will lay me some nice, fresh eggs!"

But of course, the ugly duckling did nothing of the sort.

The hen shook her head.

"You'd better start laying," she declared. "Otherwise, the old woman will put you in a pot and cook up a nice, hot stew!"

The cat laughed in a sly, mean way. "And when she does, I will chew on your bones!" she said.

The poor ugly duckling was so scared that he stopped eating altogether. He got thinner and thinner. This made the old woman very angry.

"Tomorrow, I will put you in a pot and cook up a nice, hot stew!" she told him.

That night, the old woman left the cage door open by mistake.

So the ugly duckling managed to escape… just in time.

He traveled for days, hungry and thirsty.

Finally, he found himself near a pond, in a safe bed of reeds. There was plenty to eat.

"Well," sighed the ugly duckling. "If I can't find my true family, I guess I'll just stay here, alone."

And that's what he did.

One day, he saw some beautiful birds in the sky. They were pure white, with long, graceful necks and bright orange beaks.

"How lovely they are," he thought. "I wish I could look like them. But that will never be."

When the winter came, the water in the ugly duckling's pond froze solid. There was no more food. The ugly duckling searched everywhere in the snow for something to eat. But he could find nothing.

Finally, he gave up. He lay down in the snow, tired and cold.

But then a kind farmer found him. He picked up the ugly duckling.

"Poor thing," the farmer said. "You are almost frozen. I will take you home. My children and I will take care of you."

The farmer wrapped the ugly duckling in his coat and carried him home. And he was as good as his word. He and his family cared for the duckling all winter long.

When springtime came, the ugly duckling was much better. And since the farmer's children were constantly feeding him treats, he had grown much bigger.

"It's time to set you free," the farmer told him. He put the duckling in a nearby pond.

The ugly duckling looked down into the water… and, oh! Looking back at him was the most magnificent bird he had ever seen!

"Could that be me?" he wondered.

Just then, three beautiful white birds landed in the water nearby.

"Why, I look like you!" the ugly duckling said.

"Of course you do," the birds replied. "You're a swan, just like us. But we've never seen you before. Where are you from?"

The ugly duckling told them his story. Now that he had found out what he was, he did not feel sad anymore.

From then on, whenever people saw him, they would say, "Look. What a beautiful swan! He's the finest of them all!"

He was no longer an ugly duckling. But he never forgot how it felt to be teased. So he was kind to every living creature for the rest of his life.

PUSS IN BOOTS

Once upon a time, the old man who owned the mill in town died. He left the mill to his oldest son, his donkey to his second son, and his cat to his youngest son. The oldest son kept the mill. The middle son went off with the donkey to find his fortune.

The youngest son sat down on a rock and shook his head.

"A cat? A cat?" he sighed. "What can I do with a cat?"

The cat heard his words.

"Leave everything to me," the cat told the young man. "Give me a cloak, a hat with a feather in it, a bag, and a pair of boots, and I will make your fortune."

The son did as the cat asked. After all, he had nothing to lose.

The cat caught a fat rabbit. Then he went to the castle of the king.

"Sire, the famous Marquis of Carabas sends you this fine rabbit," he said.

The next day, the cat returned to the king with some partridges.

"With the compliments of the Marquis of Carabas," he said, bowing low.

In the days that followed, the cat returned regularly. He always had gifts of delicious wild game for the king, all in the name of the Marquis of Carabas. The king and queen began to think that this Marquis was a very fine gentleman indeed.

"Is your master handsome?" the queen asked the cat, who had become known as Puss in Boots.

"Oh, yes," replied Puss in Boots. "And rich, too."

Oh, dear! Puss in Boots' owner isn't rich! Did Puss in Boots lie? Do you think it was okay? Why?

One day, the cat heard that the king, queen, and princess were taking a carriage ride that very afternoon.

The cat rushed home. "Master!" he cried. "You must go to the river this very day."

They went to the river together, and when the king's carriage appeared, the cat pushed the young man into the water.

"Help!" cried Puss in Boots. "The Marquis of Carabas is drowning!"

The king heard his cries and sent men to help. They rescued the young man and gave him new clothes to wear.

"Wouldn't you like to marry such a handsome young man?" the queen whispered to her daughter. And the princess had to agree.

"But is he rich enough?" the queen wondered.

"He is rich indeed," Puss in Boots told her. "He owns all this land and that castle yonder. Come see for yourself!"

The cat raced on ahead.

"If anyone asks who your master is," he shouted to the peasants working in the field, "you must answer 'the Marquis of Carabas'!"

And when the king's carriage passed, that's what the peasants said.

Puss in Boots raced to the castle. It was owned by a cruel giant.

The cat knocked, and the giant opened the door.

"I have heard of your great power," said the clever cat. "I understand that you can change into a lion or an elephant."

"That is true," said the giant.

"Well, I made a bet with some friends of mine," the cat went on. "They said you might be able to turn yourself into large things, but not small things. Small things, like mice, are trickier."

"Oh, yeah? Then look at this!" said the giant. And he turned himself into a mouse.

In a flash, Puss in Boots caught the mouse and gobbled him up. Then he dashed to the castle gate. He was just in time to greet the king, the queen, and the princess.

"Welcome to the castle of the Marquis of Carabas!" said Puss in Boots.

The princess looked at the new Marquis. He looked at her. And before too long, they were married.

"Now, aren't you glad you left everything to me?" said Puss in Boots.

THE PEASANT, THE SNAKE, AND THE FOX

Once upon a time, there was a peasant. He was walking home after a hard day's work when he heard a voice.

"Help, help!" the voice called. "I'm underneath this big rock. Please move it and let me out!"

"Who are you?" the peasant asked.

"I am a snake," the voice replied.

"A snake?" the peasant said. "But if I let you out, you will bite me."

"No, no, I promise I won't!" said the snake.

So the peasant moved the rock, and out darted a snake. It immediately tried to bite him.

"Why did you do that?" the man cried, jumping back.

"Because every good deed is rewarded by an evil one," the snake replied.

"I don't believe that," said the peasant.

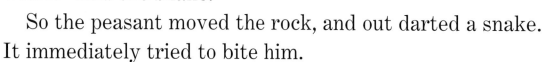

"Very well," said the snake. "Let's go ask someone. If he agrees with you, I'll go on my way. If he says I'm right, I shall bite you. Agreed?"

"Agreed," said the peasant.

A little while later, they came upon an old, lame horse.

"Friend," the peasant asked him. "If someone does a good deed, what does he get as his reward?"

"A bad deed," the horse replied. "Look at me. I served my master faithfully for years. And now that I'm old, he's left me to starve."

"Now I'll bite you!" said the snake to the peasant.

"Wait!" said the man. "One question isn't enough. We must ask someone else."

"You will get the same answer," said the snake. But he agreed.

Why do you think snakes bite?

They traveled a little way. Then they asked a sheep the same question. He, too, agreed with the horse.

"I give my master my wool," he said, "and in return, he shears me in winter, so I feel the cold. And he lets my fleece grow in the summer, so I feel hot."

"Get ready for my bite!" said the snake.

"Please! We've asked two times," the peasant said. "The last time will be the deciding one."

"All right," said the snake.

As they traveled a little way more, the peasant saw a fox in the woods. Then he had an idea. He excused himself for a moment, left the snake on the road, and went to talk to the fox.

"If you answer that a good deed is rewarded by a good deed," the peasant said, "I will give you a piglet, a lamb, or a goose."

"All right," said the fox.

The peasant went back to the snake. "Let us ask that fox over there," he said.

And so they did.

The fox answered that a good deed is always rewarded by a good deed. Then he went on, "Why ask me that question?"

"Because after I helped this snake escape from his hole under a rock, he tried to bite me," the peasant explained.

"Snakes can slither anywhere they choose," the fox said. "Why did he need your help?"

"It was a big boulder," said the snake. "Come and see!"

And he showed the fox the boulder.

The fox shook his head. "A snake like you couldn't get into such a little hole," he said.

"Of course I could!" said the snake. And he slithered into the hole to show the fox.

"Quick!" shouted the fox to the peasant. "Roll the boulder over him!" And the peasant did so, imprisoning the snake under the rock.

"Thank you, fox!" said the peasant.

"It was nothing," said the fox. "Don't forget the piglet, the lamb, or the goose you promised me!"

But when the fox came to the farm later to get his reward, the peasant chased him away.

"Well, the snake was right," the fox sighed. And off he went, with his tail between his legs.

 *Was the fox rewarded with a good deed or a bad deed? Would you have treated the fox differently? Why?*

THE LITTLE TIN SOLDIER

Once upon a time, there was a little tin soldier with only one leg.
He lived with the other toys in the house of a little boy.

The little boy played with his tin soldiers every day. He didn't
know that each night, the soldiers—and the other toys—came to life.

The little tin soldier loved to talk to the pretty tin ballerina.

The cruel Jack-in-the-box would laugh at him.

"She's not interested in you!" he would say. "You're just a little
tin soldier with one leg!"

But he was wrong. The ballerina was in love with the tin soldier.
And he loved her, too.

One day, the boy put the tin soldier on the windowsill.
"You must guard the house!" he said.
The soldier stayed there day and night, night and day, day and night.
The boy had forgotten all about the soldier.

 *The tin soldier must have missed his toy friends. What do you do to feel better when you miss your friends?*

One night, there was a terrible storm. A wind blew in the window, and the little tin soldier fell out and onto the ground outside. He landed with his bayonet stuck in the earth.

The next day, he was found by two boys.

"Too bad he only has one leg," one of them said. "Or I'd take him home."

"Let's take him anyway!" said the other. And he picked up the tin soldier and put him in his pocket.

It had rained very hard, and water rushed down the street into the drain. The boys spotted a little paper boat floating in a puddle.

"Let's put the soldier in the boat!" one of them said. "He can be a sailor!"

So the boys put the soldier in the paper boat.

The water swirled into the sewer, and the little tin soldier was carried down the drain.

Rats watched him as he sailed into the sewer, gnashing their teeth.

But the little tin soldier didn't mind. He was very brave.

The water swirled on and on until it flowed out into a river.

The boat overturned, and the tin soldier sank to the bottom of the sea.

"Oh, dear!" he thought. "I will never see my sweet ballerina again!"

Just then, a huge fish swallowed the little tin soldier.

Soon after, the fish was caught up in a fisherman's net. It ended up in a basket, brought to market.

The fish was bought by a cook. The cook worked in the very same house where the little tin soldier used to live!

"This fish will be perfect for supper," she thought. She took it home and cleaned it. And there, in its belly, she found the little tin soldier!

"He looks just like one of our boy's tin soldiers," the cook thought. So she ran downstairs to show the boy.

The boy was amazed. "It is my tin soldier!" he cried. "He must have had some amazing adventures after he fell off the windowsill."

The boy carefully put the little tin soldier on the mantel—right next to the tin ballerina!

The little tin soldier and the ballerina were very happy to be close to each other once again.

At night, they talked about what had happened to them when they were apart. The little tin soldier told the ballerina of his adventures.

"You were very brave," she said.

But fate had something else in store for them.

One day, a gust of wind blew in the window. And it blew the lovely tin ballerina off the mantel!

Oh, no! Do you think the tin soldier was scared for the ballerina? What can he do to help her? What would you do?

The tin ballerina fell and fell… until she fell into the fireplace!

The little tin soldier knew that the fire was hot. He knew he had to save the ballerina. You see, tin melts in a fire.

The little tin soldier rocked back and forth on his one leg. He rocked and rocked and finally fell into the fire as well.

He fell so close to the little ballerina that, as they started to melt, their bases melted together.

But luckily, just in time, the boy saw them and rescued them!

And ever since, the little tin solder and the ballerina have remained happily together.

THE ELVES AND THE SHOEMAKER

Once upon a time, there was a poor shoemaker. He was old, and he could no longer see very well. Because of this, his work was not as good as it had been.

One night, he put out some leather to make a pair of new shoes for a customer.

When he awoke in the morning, the shoes were made! And they were so beautiful that the customer paid twice the price that they had agreed on.

That night, the shoemaker put out more leather.

And the same thing happened!

Another beautiful pair of shoes awaited him the next morning. This time, the customer paid him three times what he had asked.

This happened many more times, till the shoemaker and his wife had saved up a good deal of money.

"Let's stay up tonight," said the shoemaker's curious wife one day, "and see what is going on."

At midnight, the shoemaker and his wife saw two elves sneak into the shop and make a pair of shoes. They were dressed in ragged clothes and shivered as they worked.

"They look so cold," the shoemaker's wife said. So the next day, she made two tiny red jackets and little red hats for the elves.

"This way, they will be warm," she said. "We should repay them for the fine work they have done!"

When the elves found the jackets and hats, they danced with joy. "With these jackets, we are rich," they laughed. "We never need to work again!"

The elves never made another pair of shoes. But luckily, the shoemaker and his wife had saved all the money they had been paid. So they lived happily the rest if their days.

THE TAIL OF THE BEAR

Once upon a time, there was a fisherman. He would go fishing every day. And then he would put the fish in a cart and travel around, selling them to his customers.

One day, a fox saw the fish on the fisherman's cart. They smelled delicious. So the fox quietly jumped onto the cart and knocked a basket of fish down onto the snow.

The fox was just about to begin her meal when a bear appeared.

"How did you get those fish?" the bear asked, his mouth watering.

The fox knew that if she didn't get rid of the bear, she'd have to share her fish. So, quickly, she said, "I've been fishing."

"Fishing?" said the bear. "How? The lake is frozen over!"

"With my tail," replied the fox. "I made a hole in the lake and stuck my tail in the hole. Soon, I felt a bite. And I pulled out these two fish!"

The bear was hungry, so he decided to try it.

He went to the lake, and made a hole in the ice.

Then he sat down with his tail in the water and waited.

It grew darker and colder.

The ice froze around the bear's tail.

Suddenly, the bear felt a bite. He pulled with all his might.

He pulled so hard that he pulled his tail right off! It had been stuck in the ice.

Ever since then, bears have had little stumps of tails instead of long, bushy ones.

JACK AND THE BEANSTALK

Once upon a time, there was a poor widow. She lived with her son, Jack, in a little cottage. They were very poor, and all they had was a milking cow.

When the cow grew old, the mother sent Jack to town to sell it. "Get a good price for it!" she told him.

On his way to town, Jack met a stranger.

"I will give you five magic beans for your cow," he told Jack.

Jack thought this was an amazing bargain. So he took the beans and gave the stranger the cow.

When Jack returned home, his mother was furious.

"You sold our only cow for a handful of beans?" she shouted. "We needed the money to buy a calf! Now we are even poorer than before!"

In a rage, she threw the magic beans out the window. Then she sent Jack to bed without his supper.

Actually, she had no supper, either. They were that poor.

The next day, when Jack went outside, he saw an amazing sight.

There, just by the cottage window, was a beanstalk.

It was gigantic, and it reached far into the clouds.

"Those beans really must have been magic!" Jack thought.

"I wonder where the beanstalk goes?" Jack thought. So he decided to climb it and find out.

He climbed and climbed. Finally, he rose above the clouds.

And there, he saw a huge castle of gray stone.

"I wonder who lives in the castle!" he thought.

When he got to the castle, Jack knocked and knocked. But no one heard him. So he pushed open the door and went inside.

"What are you doing here?" a giant voice thundered.

Jack looked up.

And there, standing in the doorway, was the largest woman Jack had ever seen!

"Please, ma'am," he said, "I am hungry and thirsty."

The giant woman was not unkind. "Come in," she told Jack. "I will give you a bowl of milk. But be careful of my husband, the giant. He eats children like you."

Jack was very frightened. But he was also hungry. So he went with the giant's wife.

The milk was very good. Jack was just finishing it when the giant woke up.

"Fee fi fo fum! I smell the blood of an Englishman!" the giant shouted.

"Quick!" said the giant's wife. "Hide in the oven!"

And that's exactly what Jack did.

"Do I smell a child?" the giant asked his wife.

"Oh, fah," said his wife. "You're always smelling children. Sit down and I'll make you dinner."

The giant sat down at the table. He opened a jug of wine and began to drink.

Then he had his dinner.

After dinner, he counted all his gold pieces. After a little while, his eyes began to close. Soon he fell asleep and started to snore.

Jack sneaked out of the oven. But before he left the castle, he filled a little bag with gold pieces and took them with him.

He tiptoed past the snoring giant. "I hope he doesn't hear me!" he thought.

Do you think the giant will hear Jack? Will he get home safely?

Jack raced across the clouds to the beanstalk. He climbed down it as fast as his legs could carry him.

When he got to the bottom, he called for his mother. She raced to the beanstalk.

Jack showed her the bag of gold.

"Mother, we are rich!" he said happily. "You see, I did the right thing, selling the cow for those magic beans."

In the days that followed, Jack and his mother fixed up the cottage and bought many things they had never had before.

But soon, the last gold piece was spent.

Jack decided to go back up the beanstalk to see if he could find some more.

This time, Jack sneaked into the castle without meeting up with the giant's wife. He went straight to the oven and hid inside.

Soon after, the giant came into the room. He began to sniff.

"Fee fi fo fum! I smell the blood of an Englishman!" he shouted.

But since his wife had seen no one come in, she paid no attention.

Just as before, the giant drank his wine and ate his dinner. But then, he took a hen out and put her on the table. "Lay!" he commanded. And the hen laid a golden egg!

Jack saw this from a crack in the oven door. "I want that hen!" he decided.

Soon, the giant fell asleep. Then Jack jumped out of the oven, grabbed the hen, and raced to the beanstalk.

This time, though, the squawking of the hen woke the giant up.

"Thief! Thief!" the giant shouted. He and his wife chased after Jack.

But Jack made it safely down the beanstalk.

When Jack returned home, his mother was waiting for him. "Is that all you stole?" she asked. "A hen?"

"Just wait," Jack told her. And before long, the hen laid a golden egg.

Jack's mother was very happy!

Jack and his mother found themselves very wealthy indeed. They had everything they needed and more.

But soon, Jack's mother grew ill. Nothing would make her happy. Jack called in all the doctors in the land, but no one could help her.

"What if I went back to the giant's castle?" Jack thought. "It is a magic castle. Maybe there, I could find some magic that would help my mother."

He was afraid, but he loved his mother very much. So he was determined to climb the tall beanstalk one last time.

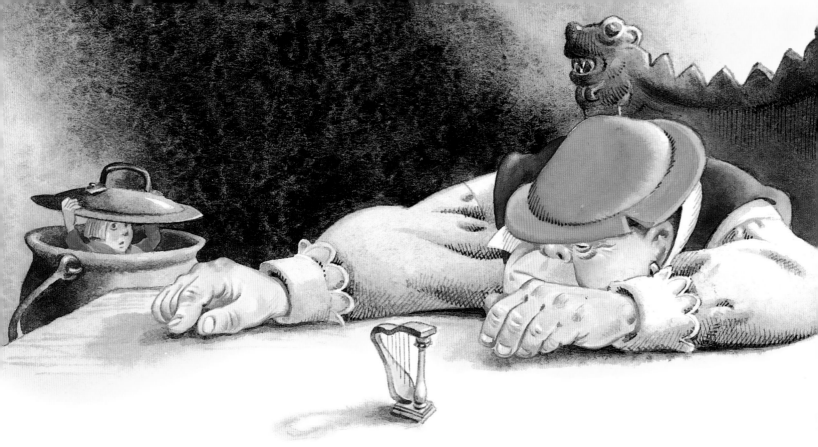

This time, he sneaked into the giant's castle through the window. Again, he hid in the oven. And again, the giant came into the kitchen and shouted: "Fee fi fo fum! I smell the blood of an Englishman!"

This time, after dinner, the giant took out a little gold harp. "Sing!" commanded the giant. And the harp played and sang the most beautiful, soothing music Jack had ever heard.

Do you know what a harp is? How does it sound? How might this harp help Jack's sick mother?

When the giant was snoring, Jack crept out of the oven, picked up the harp, and raced out of the castle.

Then the harp cried out, "Master! Master! Wake up! A thief is taking me away!"

The giant awoke and started to chase Jack.

Jack raced to the beanstalk and started to slide down.

But the beanstalk began to shake!

The giant was climbing down, too!

"Mother! Mother!" Jack cried. "Bring me an ax!"

His mother quickly brought an ax, and Jack began to chop at the beanstalk.

The frightened giant then scurried back up the beanstalk—just before the beanstalk came crashing down.

The soothing music of the magic harp soon cured Jack's mother of her illness. The hen kept laying golden eggs. And Jack and his mother lived happily from that day on.

THE EMPEROR'S NEW CLOTHES

Once upon a time, there was a very rich emperor who only cared about how he looked. He loved his fine clothes and would change them every hour.

It happened that two scoundrels had heard of the emperor's vanity. They decided to take advantage of him, and they came up with a plan.

First, they went to the palace.

"We are two very famous tailors," they told the palace guard. "After many years of work, we have invented a cloth that is exquisitely light and fine. In fact," they went on, "it is invisible to anyone who is too stupid to appreciate its fine quality."

The chief of the guards told this story to the court chamberlain.

The chamberlain told the prime minister. The prime minister told the emperor.

The emperor was very curious. So he decided to see the two tailors.

"Your Highness," they told him, "this cloth will be very beautiful. We will weave it especially for you, and it will be the most exquisite cloth in the kingdom!"

The emperor gave the two men a bag of gold and told them to start weaving the cloth right away.

The scoundrels asked for a loom and silk and gold thread.

Then they measured the emperor for his beautiful new suit of clothes.

They promised they would be done in one week.

Do you think there is such a thing as invisible cloth? What would happen if you wore clothes made from such cloth?

A few days later, the curious emperor sent his prime minister to see how the work was going.

"Everything is fine!" said the two scoundrels. "Look! I am sure that you are refined enough to see the beautiful colors. And feel how soft it is!"

The prime minister bent over the loom. But of course, he could see nothing… for there was nothing there.

He trembled. "If I see nothing, that means I'm stupid!" he thought. "And if the emperor finds out, I will lose my job!"

So he pretended to admire the cloth. "It is certainly marvelous," he said. "I will tell the emperor."

Soon, the scoundrels went to the emperor. In their arms, they held… nothing at all.

"Your Highness," they said, "look. Here is the suit. Is it not beautiful? Do the colors not sparkle in the light?"

The emperor stared and stared. He felt his palms grow damp. He could not see a thing! And if he could not see the clothes... then he must be stupid! And if he was stupid... then he should not be emperor!

So he decided to pretend to see the suit. And of course, everyone around him decided to pretend exactly the same thing!

The two scoundrels helped the emperor put on the suit of clothes. Of course, the emperor had nothing on at all. But no one would tell him.

The people of the kingdom had heard about the amazing suit. They wanted to see it. So the emperor called for his carriage, and he rode through the town, showing off his new clothes.

Of course, no one saw the clothes. But all the people were too afraid to admit it. They thought *other* people would think they were stupid. So they pretended to see the clothes.

"Look at how beautiful they are!" said one.

"The colors of the fabric are lovely, aren't they?" said another.

Just as the scoundrels had thought, no one was willing to admit that the emperor had nothing on!

But then a small child, who saw things as they were, went over to the carriage.

"The emperor has nothing on!" he shouted, laughing.

The people in the crowd repeated the boy's remark.

"He has nothing on! The emperor has nothing on!" they whispered to one another. And they all realized it was true.

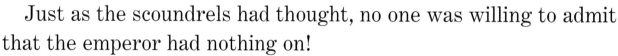

So did the emperor. But of course, he couldn't admit it. So he continued to ride in his carriage. And the two scoundrels got away with their gold.

 It can be hard to admit when you're wrong. What would you do if you knew you were wrong about something?

SIX ABLE MEN

Once upon a time, there was a young soldier named Martin.

For many years, he fought in a war for his king. Finally, the war was over.

The king told Martin to guard a bridge. Then the king went back to his castle, forgetting all about poor Martin.

After two years, Martin decided it was time to visit the king to get his back pay. So he set off for the palace.

Soon he came to a stream. Sitting near it was a very large man with a very soft voice.

"Would you like to get across?" the man asked.

"Yes, please," said Martin.

So the large man uprooted a tree and laid it across the stream like a bridge.

Martin was so impressed that he asked the man to travel with him, and the man agreed.

The two traveled a bit further when they came upon a man with a rifle.

"What are you shooting at?" Martin asked.

"That spider in the web on that hill over there," the man replied. The hill was almost a mile away.

When the three men walked to the hill, Martin found a spider's web with a hole in the middle and no spider.

Martin was so impressed that he asked the man to travel with him, and the man agreed.

The three men walked and walked. Soon they came to a windmill that went round and round. But there was no wind.

A little down the road, they found a fat man who was blowing at the windmill out of one nostril. He explained that he was so strong that he could sneeze up a hurricane.

Martin was so impressed that he asked the man to travel with him, and the man agreed.

The four men next came upon a man with his legs tied together. "Why are you tied up?" Martin asked.

"I am so quick," the man explained, "that if I don't tie my legs up, I run as fast as the wind, and cannot enjoy the scenery. Everyone calls me Fastfoot."

Martin was so impressed that he asked the man to travel with him, and the man agreed.

The five then came upon a man with a round face who sat under a tree. "If I straighten my hat," he told them, "I will freeze everything around me."

Martin was so impressed that he asked the man to travel with him, and the man agreed.

The six men finally reached the royal city. There was a notice hanging on the gate. It said that whoever could beat the princess in a race could marry her.

Martin decided to challenge the princess. But he said that one of his servants would run in his place. The princess agreed.

The day of the race, Fastfoot untied his legs and took off. Each of the runners had to fill a jug of water at a stream and bring it back to the finish line. After Fastfoot filled his jug, he decided to take a nap.

He slept and slept.

When the princess caught up with him, she overturned his jug. "Now he will never catch me!" she thought.

But the farsighted hunter noticed that Fastfoot was asleep. He shot and hit a spot near Fastfoot's ear, waking him up.

When Fastfoot realized what had happened, he raced back to the stream, refilled the jug, and beat the princess to the finish line.

Now, the king had no intention of letting a poor soldier marry his daughter. So he invited Martin and his friends to the palace.

He took them into a dining room for a meal. But the dining room was really a trap. The king locked the door. Then he lit a great fire underneath the room. "None of them will survive," he thought.

 How do you think Martin and his friends will escape from the hot room?

The room got hotter and hotter. But Martin did not panic. He straightened the hat of the round-faced man. Soon, the room was freezing.

But the king was still determined not to let Martin marry the princess.

The king offered Martin a large sum of money if he gave up the wedding.

"You can take as much of my gold and riches as you can carry," he said.

Martin agreed.

The king didn't know the strength of Martin's strongest friend. He filled a bag with his entire fortune, and still the man could carry it. So when Martin and his friends left the city, they were very rich… and the king was very poor.

The king realized he had been tricked. So he sent his army to bring his treasure back.

The soldiers soon caught up with Martin and demanded that he return the king's gold and jewels.

This time, the fat man began to blow. And the soldiers and their horses simply blew away!

Martin and his friends divided the king's treasure equally among them. And they all lived happily ever after!

Martin's friends can do many strange things. If you could choose one funny or strange thing you could do, what would it be?

THE SEVEN CROWS

Once upon a time, a mother, a father, and their eight children lived in a little cottage in the mountains. Seven of the children were boys, and the youngest was a girl.

The girl was the sweetest child you could hope to meet. But the boys were always being naughty and getting into mischief.

One day, the boys did a terrible thing.

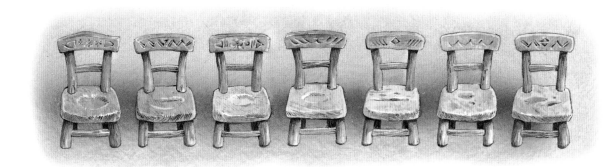

A dangerous grass grew in a field nearby. Their father had told them never to feed it to the animals.

But on this day, the boys picked the grass and added it to the animals' feed.

Soon, the family's few goats and cows fell ill. Their bellies ached and they couldn't stand up.

"We won't have any milk!" moaned the mother. "We won't be able to make cheese! How will we eat?"

The sons just laughed, not realizing the evil they had done.

"Better to have given birth to seven crows rather than to seven sons!" the mother cried in despair.

A dark cloud slipped over the sun. An ill wind blew. And, like magic, her seven sons turned into seven crows! They flew away, cawing as they went.

The woman was very sad and frightened. So was her husband. And their little daughter suffered most of all, for she had loved her brothers dearly.

Time passed. Finally, the girl decided she must go in search of her brothers.

Her mother cried and cried, but the girl felt she had to try.

She left the cottage. She searched for days and days. Her clothes grew tattered and torn.

Finally, she came to a strange little cottage on a hill. It looked gloomy and sad, but she felt drawn to it —so she went inside.

There, she found a table with seven bowls on it. Could she have found the home of her brothers?

She was very hungry, so she took a little food in one of the bowls. Then she went upstairs. There were seven little beds in the bedroom. She fell onto one of them and soon was fast asleep.

Later on, seven chattering crows pushed open the front door.
"Someone has been here!" said one, seeing the dirty bowl.

The crows went upstairs… and there was their little sister, asleep!

At that moment, the girl opened her eyes. "Brothers!" she cried happily, reaching out her arms. "I've found you! You must come home with me," she told the crows. "Our mother and father miss you so!"

"But don't we disgust you?" one crow asked sadly.

"Of course not," said his sister. "You are my brothers, and I love you."

"We would like to come back," another said.

"Then you shall!" said the girl.

> *Have you ever forgiven someone? How did it make you feel?*

The crows gathered their possessions, including some sparkly stones (for crows love to gather things that glitter).

Then they picked up their sister and flew toward their home.

At first she was frightened. But her brothers held her carefully. And the view was lovely from up in the clouds.

Soon, the crows landed in their yard. "Mother, come see!" called the girl.

When their mother came out of the cottage, she was overjoyed.

"My sons!" she cried. "I am so happy to see you!"

Their father, too, was delighted to have his sons home.

It turned out that the sparkly stones were diamonds and rubies.

And this treasure allowed the family to live happily for many a year.

ROBINSON AND THE GIANT

Once upon a time, there was a little white mouse named Robinson. Robinson was very brave… and very, very curious. Because Robinson was so curious, he had many adventures.

Every now and then, he would disappear for a day or two.

"Where have you been?" everyone would ask him.

"Exploring," he would say.

These are the stories of his explorations.

Robinson lived in the woods with his friends, the other woodland creatures and the little gnomes. One day, he was wandering at the edge of the forest when he came upon a giant castle.

"I wonder who lives here?" he thought. He pushed open the giant door.

Inside, the first thing Robinson saw was a table. On the table were a basket of apples and a basket of cherries.

Hungry as usual, Robinson climbed up to the basket and started to eat the cherries.

Suddenly, he heard the sound of giant footsteps. "I'd better hide!" he thought. But

in his hurry to get down from the table, he knocked over the pepper shaker… and started to sneeze.

"I hear you!' shouted a giant voice. "Trying to steal my cherries, are you?"

The giant entered the room, spotted Robinson, and made a grab for him.

"Please don't hurt me!" Robinson cried. "I only ate two cherries."

"Hurt you?" the giant laughed. "I won't hurt you. I just want to know who you are and what you're doing here."

Robinson was reassured. So he told the giant who he was and how much he liked cherries.

"Well, my name is George," the giant said. "And I like cherries too… and apples. So let's pick them all up and eat them together!"

And that is how Robinson made friends with the giant George.

Robinson and George are very different, but they are still friends. How are your friends different from you?

GEORGE HELPS OUT

When Robinson returned to his friends in the woods, he told them all about meeting the giant.

"How big is he?" asked Auntie Mouse.

"He's taller than our mill!" said Robinson.

"Taller than the mill?" Ferret gasped.

"Yes," Robinson said. "Why don't I invite him for a visit, and you'll see for yourselves?"

So Robinson mailed an invitation to George.

When the mailman delivered the invitation, George was very pleased.

"Let's go," he told the mailman, "and I will give you a ride back to the mill."

Soon, George arrived for his visit.

George had to be very careful where he placed his feet so as not to step on someone or ruin something.

"See?" Robinson told his friends. "I told you how big he was. Look!"

And it was true. George was taller than the windmill (with his hat on, of course).

When George saw the windmill, he had an idea.

He blew and he blew. The blades of the windmill turned and turned, faster than ever. Soon, all the grain in the mill was turned into flour.

Squirrel, who owned the mill, was very pleased.

"I would like to give you a gift for helping us," she said.

Squirrel asked the painter gnome to paint a portrait of George.

It was a beautiful painting. It showed George in the village, sitting next to the little houses of Robinson and his friends.

Everyone agreed that the portrait made George look very handsome... and very big!

George took the painting home and hung it in his castle.

If you were to give a picture as a gift, what would you draw or color or paint? Whom would you give it to? Why?

GEORGE AND THE TORNADO

The next day, the sky darkened. The clouds grew thick and gray.

Soon, a tornado whirled through the forest. It knocked down trees. It ripped off doors and windows in the castle.

"It will be a lot of work to repair everything," George sighed.

Suddenly he had a terrible thought. What had the tornado done to the homes of his new friends? "I must go see," he said.

Indeed, many of his friends' homes had been destroyed.

"Are you all right?" George asked.

"We are," Beaver told him. "And we will soon rebuild our homes. But the trees have been destroyed, and it takes many years to grow new ones."

"Maybe I can help," said George.

George took away the old, broken trees. He brought them back to his castle, where he used them for firewood.

When he came back, he was carrying three new, big trees!

"These came from the forest over the mountain," he explained.

He dug nice, deep holes in the ground where the old trees had been.

He carefully planted the trees in the holes, and then went back for more.

His forest friends watched in amazement.

Soon, there were healthy trees all around.

"Don't forget to water them," he reminded everyone.

Have you ever planted anything? What does a plant need besides water to grow?

After all the trees were planted, there was a party to celebrate the new trees.

"Hooray for George!" Robinson and his friends cheered.

"Thank you," said George. "Next time, you must visit me in my castle." He waved good-bye.

Robinson was very proud to have such a wonderful giant for a friend!

GEORGE'S CASTLE

One day, George came to the forest to invite everyone to lunch.

They were all very excited.

"We shouldn't eat for three days before we go," said Rabbit to Frog.

"Why?" asked Frog.

"If you are invited to lunch at a giant's house, surely the lunch will be giant, too!" Rabbit explained.

"That's true," said Mole. "But even if the giant has lots to eat, there are a lot of us to feed!"

The big day came. It was a long hike to the castle. So everyone was very hungry when they finally got there.

After George welcomed them and showed them all around the castle, he took them into the dining room.

What a wonderful sight met their eyes!

George had set up many little tables on top of his giant one. Lunch was delicious. And there was plenty of food to go around!

They all had a marvelous time. (George was a very good cook!)

After the meal, Robinson stood on a salt shaker and made a long speech.

He thanked George for the delicious lunch. And he thanked the giant for being their friend.

George was very moved.

Then the Magic Gnome made a speech. And then Beaver did. And then Rabbit wanted to say something, too.

By the time the speeches were over, it was quite late.

"You must stay the night!" George said.

> *All the forest folk are going to sleep at the castle. Have you ever had a sleepover? What fun things do you do at a sleepover?*

So all the forest folk stayed in the castle of George the giant. They had all eaten well, and they were all very sleepy.

"Someday, we will tell our grandchildren that we slept in a giant's castle!" said Mother Mouse, stretching.

Robinson yawned. It had been a wonderful day.
And he knew there would be more wonderful days to come!

FROG'S RAFT

One day, Robinson's friend, Frog, decided that he wanted to explore the river from end to end.

So he built himself a nice paper boat and set out to see what he could see.

Now, if you've ever sailed a paper boat, you know that paper gets very, very wet.

And besides getting wet from the river, this paper boat was also caught in a rainstorm.

Soon, it sank to the bottom of the river. But this gave Frog an idea.

"I'll build a boat so big and strong that it will never sink," he said. "In fact, I'll build a house that floats. That way, I'll be able to travel up and down the river, living where I please and going anywhere I want!"

He asked the three Mouse brothers if they would help.

Of course, they agreed. After all, what are friends for?

When they heard what Frog was doing, many of his friends came to help.

Auntie Mouse made some refreshments.

Everyone worked very hard to help Frog.

After all, that's what friends do!

Before long, the floating house was almost ready.

Frog couldn't wait to get started.

Do you think it would be fun to live in a house that floats? Are there special things you could do if you lived in a floating house?

After he had thanked his friends for their hard work, he brought his floating house out to the middle of the river.

This was no paper boat. The floating house was very strong. It would not sink.

"Good-bye!" the Mouse brothers called. "Good luck! Have a nice trip!"

And that was how Frog began his life on the river.

Frog was happy. It was wonderful to have a floating house that could take him down the river.

One day, he saw a bottle stuck in the mud near the river bank.

Frog decided to throw a rope over the bottle. He tied his floating house to the bottle, so that the house would come to a rest.

Then he stretched out on deck and took a nap.

Suddenly, Frog heard someone calling his name.

It was the Mouse brothers and Auntie Mouse.

"We wanted to find out how you were getting on," they told Frog. "We've been following you all day."

"Well, come aboard!" Frog said. "You are very welcome!"

The mice admired Frog's wonderful house. Then one Mouse brother noticed the bottle.

"Why, we could climb into that bottle and look at the bottom of the river!" he realized.

Two of the Mouse brothers lowered themselves into the bottle, using a long, strong vine. Frog and Auntie Mouse helped.

Soon, the brothers were down in their new underwater observatory.

"How amazing it is down here!" they called up to Frog. "We can see snails, and fish, and water beetles, and plants!"

In an aquarium, you can see fish swimming underwater. Have you ever been to an aquarium? What do you think fish do underwater all day?

It was a very warm day. After their adventure underwater, the Mouse brothers felt hot and sticky.

Then, Frog had an idea.

He took some planks and drilled some holes in them.

Then he put the plank under a waterfall.

It made a perfect shower for the Mouse brothers.

The water was refreshing but a little chilly.

Living on the river was fun, the Mouse brothers decided. But they were happier in their nice, dry house on nice, dry land!

THE SIX LITTLE GUESTS

Every Monday afternoon, Auntie Mouse went with her wheelbarrow to buy supplies at the big store in the town square.

One day, while she was in town, she saw her friend, the doctor's wife, and her six children.

"I wonder if she has moved into her new house yet," Auntie Mouse thought.

"Unfortunately, the new house isn't ready yet," the doctor's wife told Auntie Mouse. "They are still finishing the kitchen floor. So tonight, we'll have to get a sandwich somewhere."

"Why don't you come to dinner at my house?" Auntie Mouse said. "I'm making rice soup, and there's always enough to go around!"

"Yay!" cried one of the little mice. "We're going to dinner at Auntie Mouse's house!" The little mouse knew that there were always good things to eat at Auntie Mouse's.

"Are you sure it's no trouble?" asked the doctor's wife.

"Of course not," said Auntie Mouse. "Everything I need is right here in the store. It will be a pleasure!"

Have you ever had rice soup?
What's your favorite soup?

That night, Auntie Mouse fed the hungry little mice bowls and bowls of her delicious rice soup.

"Thank you for inviting us," said the doctor's wife.

She and Auntie Mouse did the dishes. Then they sat down in the kitchen to talk while the six little mice played in the parlor.

Suddenly, the doctor's wife looked up.

"Oh, dear! I hadn't realized how late it was getting," she said.

"You must stay here tonight," Auntie Mouse insisted. "It isn't safe for you to travel through the woods in the dark."

There weren't enough beds for all the little mice. So Auntie Mouse pulled out the drawers of all her dressers, and put soft pillows and blankets inside. They made wonderful beds.

Auntie Mouse and the doctor's wife talked quietly at the table. "Thank you for letting us stay," the doctor's wife said. "When our house is ready, you must come for a long visit!"

Soon, the little mice were fast asleep.

CROCUS THE ASTRONOMER

Crocus was one of the gnomes who lived with Robinson and the other woodland creatures in the forest.

There was one thing he loved more than anything in the world. Crocus loved looking at the stars.

Every night, he would take his telescope and go to the top of the hill, where there weren't many trees. Then he would stare at the stars for many hours.

One night, he felt a little sleepy. So he decided to take a nap.

But he was not alone.

In the forest were a group of tiny creatures—even tinier than the gnomes and the mice and the squirrels. They were elves. And they were very mischievous. They loved to play tricks on people.

And they had decided to play a trick on Crocus.

"Shh!" they whispered. "Don't wake Crocus!"

Then they opened the lens of Crocus's telescope.

When the elves were done with their work, one of them tickled Crocus's ear with a piece of grass to wake him up. Then they snuck away to see what would happen.

Crocus stretched. Then he peered through his telescope. But he was in for a big surprise.

"What?" Crocus was amazed. "What is that on the moon?"

Behind a tree stump, the elves laughed and laughed. Of course, they knew what was going on.

While Crocus had slept, the elves had drawn a picture on the lens of his telescope. It was a picture of a big face, sticking out its tongue.

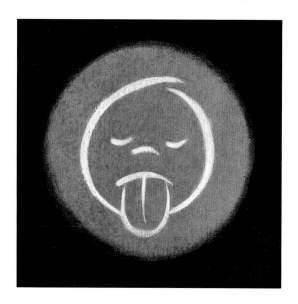

When Crocus looked at the moon through the telescope, it looked like the moon was sticking out its tongue at him!

Of course, Crocus soon realized what had happened, and cleaned his telescope.

"Silly elves!" he said to himself. For of course, he knew who had caused all the mischief.

THE STEAM MACHINE

Crocus's friend Wisteria, the blacksmith gnome, was always inventing things.

He was very clever.

One day, as he waited for the water to boil for his cup of tea, he stared and stared at the steam coming out of his kettle.

"All that steam!" he thought. "It pushes out with so much force. There must be some way to use the pressure of the steam to make something run…"

Wisteria had an idea. If he could make lots of steam, the steam could move a wheel. Then the wheel could move a machine.

He started to draw the plans. And soon he had a model of an engine—a steam engine!
—up and running.

Wisteria hooked up his steam engine to many different machines in his home.

One machine cracked nuts for him. Another made bread. A third drove a fan, so it was cool inside. And a fourth gave him a nice back rub!

Wisteria was very comfortable. He sat and read a book about inventions while he got his back rubbed.

But of course, because he was an inventor, he was never comfortable for long.

Soon, he had another idea.

"I wonder…" he thought.

What kind of inventions did Wisteria power from his steam engine?

"If the steam from my machine can make wheels turn, then I can use steam to make the wheels on a cart turn, too!" he said.

He worked and worked. And finally... his machine was ready.

Wisteria had invented a machine that could move on the ground, using the power of steam.

"And to think it all started with a cup of tea!" Wisteria said.

THE AIRPLANE

Wisteria wasn't the only inventor in the forest. Professor Mouse was interested in inventions, too.

He had once discovered that a balloon full of hot air would rise into the sky. Ever since then, he had tried to use this idea to build himself a flying machine.

The balloon worked, but not very well. Winds often blew it off course, and sometimes it would hit the tops of the trees and fall to the ground.

One day, Professor Mouse watched Frog pedal by on his bicycle. "If only I could use pedals to move forward in my balloon," he thought.

He looked up and saw a hawk flying through the air. "His wings keep him up. He floats on the air..." he thought.

Then Professor Mouse had an idea.

He built some wings... put them on a bicycle ...and invented an airplane!

His friends all cheered when they saw him fly for the first time.

Just then, Wisteria came by in his steam engine car. Black smoke belched up into the sky.

"Amazing!" said Wisteria, stopping to watch Professor Mouse in his flying machine.

Unfortunately, the smoke from Wisteria's engine drifted up to the airplane.

Professor Mouse started to cough. Then he stopped peddling. His flying machine drifted down… and crashed into Wisteria's car!

Wisteria apologized. Then, as inventors do, they started to think… and talk.

"I wonder…" said Professor Mouse.

"If we could combine…" said Wisteria.

"My invention with yours…" Professor Mouse went on.

"We could make a steam-driven airplane!" Wisteria finished.

What a brilliant idea!

So the two went off to work on it together.

And for all we know, they are working on it still!

> *Wisteria and Professor Mouse came up with a new idea by working together. Have you ever worked with a friend to make something? What was it?*

ROBINSON'S GREAT ADVENTURES

Now, as you know, Robinson loved adventures. He was always disappearing for a day or two.

But one time, he was away for a long, long while. Everyone in the forest wondered where he had gone.

"Have you seen Robinson?" they asked one another.

No one had—not Blackbird or Crow or Auntie Mouse or Mole or any of the others. Even Seagull, who flew over the ocean, hadn't seen Robinson.

All the forest creatures were very sad. They thought Robinson was gone for good.

Then, one day, after a difficult journey, he returned home again!

"He's back! He's back!" everyone shouted. "Robinson has returned!"

"Finally! Where have you been?" asked Mole.

"It was a long journey," Robinson told him.

"Where did you go?" they all asked.

"It all started," Robinson began, "when I was shipwrecked on an island. There were high, white cliffs..."

These are Robinson's stories.

> _It sounds like Robinson has been exploring again! Would you like to go exploring, too? Where would you go?_

ROBINSON AND THE PYRAMIDS

Robinson was stranded on the island. He needed to find a way to get home.

One morning, he noticed an empty eagle's nest high on a cliff.

Inside it were some eagle feathers. And they gave Robinson an idea…

He made some wings out of the feathers. Then he tried to fly off the cliff.

Remember, Robinson was very brave!

At first, the feathers seemed to be working. But Robinson was too heavy for them.

He soon found himself in the water.

The water was salty and cold. Robinson floated, holding onto a wooden stick.

Then he saw a flock of birds in the sky above him. He waved his handkerchief at them, hoping they would help.

They were kind-hearted birds. Robinson tied the handkerchief to the stick and hung on as the birds picked him up and flew into the sky. It was a long flight. But finally, they reached land.

The birds put Robinson down in the middle of a sandstorm. Robinson closed his eyes to keep the sandout. When the storm was over, he opened his eyes.

He found that he was standing near a small pyramid. In front of him were two giant pyramids.

As he sat on the tiny pyramid, trying to decide what to do, he noticed an opening in one of the pyramids.

He decided to go exploring. Maybe there would be someone inside who could help him get home again.

Inside the building was a small lamp. Robinson lit it and found himself in a marvelous room.

Clearly, the room had belonged to some people who lived long, long ago.

All around were pictures and statues. And along one of the walls was a boat.

Robinson smiled. It was exactly the kind of boat he needed! If he could drag it back to the river, he could find his way home again.

It took him all day. But he finally did it.

Robinson floated down the river. He used his handkerchief as a sail.
He raced past beautiful white buildings and tall palm trees.
Then he saw something under the water.

He leaned over to see what it was.

It was a white ball... no, two white balls. They looked like eyes
that were swimming underwater.

Robinson had never seen anything like them before.

Then he suddenly realized what they were.

They were the eyes of a crocodile!

The crocodile swam under the boat. It picked the boat up and smashed it against the shore.

The next thing Robinson knew, he was lying in some reeds at the side of the river.

Above him were two pink sticks. He grabbed ahold of them to help him sit up. But that was a mistake.

The pink sticks weren't sticks at all. They were the legs of a flamingo—a large, pink bird. And the flamingo began to fly!

What might Robinson see from high up in the sky?

Every now and then, the flamingo bent his head down to look at his little passenger. Robinson tried to tell the bird that he'd like to be put down on the ground, but the bird clearly didn't understand him.

They flew over a forest. Then Robinson saw a city. It was very big and very beautiful.

Then he saw some very strange animals, indeed! They were carrying little houses on their backs, and they had long, long noses. There were people riding the animals, too, but he couldn't see who they were.

By now, Robinson was getting very tired. He knew he would soon have to let go.

So he started to look around for a place he could land.

Soon Robinson saw a large, reddish building hidden in some trees. There were strange faces carved into the building. He wondered what the building was.

Robinson let himself go above a tall tree near the building. The leaves were nice and soft. He landed on the ground, safe and sound.

But where was he?

He decided to look around and see.

Robinson walked toward the building. Suddenly, he heard voices.

"He looks just like my grandfather!" said a voice.

He stepped inside. And there was a group of mice who looked just like him!

ROBINSON AND THE TREASURE

The only difference between Robinson and the other mice was that they had large black spots.

Robinson was very happy to see them. He explained how he had come there.

When he was finished, it was their turn to explain who they were.

"We don't know," they told him. "We have been here for a very long time. You are the first creature like us whom we've seen in many years.

"A long time ago," they told him, "some mean-looking people came here. We watched them dig a hole in the ground and bury some wooden chests. They have never returned."

"What was in the chests?" Robinson asked.

"We will show you," the mice told him.

They took Robinson through a long, dark tunnel.

What do you think was is the wooden chests?

At the end of the tunnel was a large hole.

And in the hole was an amazing treasure.

There was gold, silver, and many precious jewels.

The mice asked Robinson to choose a gift for himself. They were very kind.

Then they helped him build a new boat.

Soon he set sail for home.

But before he did, he promised to return and visit them some day.

Robinson will miss his new friends. What can he do to keep in touch with them?

THE GOLDSMITH GNOME

The day after Robinson's return, he slept very late. He did not get up until twelve o'clock.

That afternoon, he showed his friends the gift he had chosen from the spotted mice.

It was a beautiful necklace.

Everyone wanted to touch the strange necklace. But Carnation, the goldsmith gnome, was the most curious of all.

"You must have seen some amazing jewels in your travels," he said. "If you could only draw them, I could make jewelry based on your pictures."

"I can try," Robinson said.

He sat down at Carnation's work table and started to draw.

After several hours, Robinson stopped drawing. And Carnation started making jewelry from Robinson's designs.

A few days later, Robinson went back to Carnation's workshop.

There, on a table covered with a piece of blue velvet, was an amazing collection of gold necklaces, pendants, earrings, and pins.

They looked a lot like the jewels Robinson had seen during his travels.

As Robinson stared in amazement, Crocus, the magician gnome, came in.

"These are very wonderful," he said, examining them under his microscope.

"I could not have made them without Robinson," Carnation said modestly.

Everyone came to admire Carnation's work.

Then Carnation took out a beautiful gold crown. He placed it on Robinson's head.

"Robinson deserves much of the credit," Carnation said. "I hereby crown him King of the Jewels!"

Everyone clapped loudly.

Robinson wore the crown all day long. Then he carefully put it away.

"I will show it to my children one day," he said.

And perhaps he did!

If you could be King or Queen of something, what would it be?

SUNFLOWER AND PUMPKIN SEEDS

At the end of every summer, the pumpkins in the forest grew large and ripe and sweet. Each year, the Beaver family roasted these pumpkins. Then, they sold roasted pumpkin at the market.

They used a large tin drum filled with charcoal as a grill.

"How heavy this pumpkin is!" said a beaver as he rolled one of the largest pumpkins toward the grill.

Soon, you could smell the aroma of roasted pumpkin everywhere. Two Blackbird cousins came over to investigate.

"Would you mind giving us the seeds?" one of the Blackbirds asked. For they had a plan.

"Wouldn't mind at all!" said the Beavers. "We don't use the seeds. You're welcome to them."

The Blackbird cousins took the seeds to a shack deep in the woods.

The year before, they had prepared an iron barrel that rotated over a fire. Gentian, the herbalist gnome, had helped them.

They put the pumpkin seeds in the barrel. The Ants and Bumblebees helped.

Soon, the husks of the seeds popped open. The seeds inside were roasted perfectly.

This gave the Crows an idea. They brought over some sunflower seeds they gathered from the sunflower plants.

The Crows roasted the sunflower seeds in the Blackbird's machine. They were delicious.

"Mm! Roasted seeds are so much better than raw seeds!" said a Bumblebee.

The next day at the market, the Beaver family was selling their roasted pumpkin.

And for the first time, the Blackbird cousins had something to sell, too.

They were selling their roasted pumpkin seeds. They sold every single seed.

The Crows sold all their roasted sunflower seeds, too.

Everyone in the forest agreed that the roasted seeds were delicious!

THE GNOMES' PARTY

Every year, the gnomes of the forest had a party for all the forest creatures. And this year, as usual, they traveled around on their cart, weeks before the party, blowing on a bugle and beating a drum.

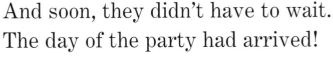

"Come one, come all to our party!" they cried.

No one could wait until the day of the party.

And soon, they didn't have to wait.

The day of the party had arrived!

The party was held in the middle of the square.

There were games to play and good things to eat.

There was even a merry-go-round!

In the middle of the square was a pole.

On top of the pole were two bags. One bag held royal jelly, made especially by the Queen Bee. It was said that one spoonful of royal jelly could satisfy your appetite for a whole week!

The other bag held two pieces of a delicious cheese that Crocus, the magician gnome, had provided.

All the animals tried to climb the pole and get the prizes. But there was grease on the pole, and it was very slippery. It was hard to climb it without sliding down!

What a fun game the animals are playing!
What are your favorite games?

The Beavers sold their famous roasted pumpkin, and the Crows sold their salted sunflower seeds. They were very good!

At the end of the day, no one had managed to climb up the pole. So the gnomes gave everyone a taste of the jelly and the delicious cheese. They all had a wonderful time.

THE ANTHILL

One day, it was very hot.

Bear was even hotter. So he decided to stretch out in a field and take a nap.

Suddenly, he felt a nip. Then he felt another.

"Ouch!" he cried. What was going on?

Poor Bear got up and ran. He ended up in Mole's hole.

"What's the matter?" Mole asked.

"Ants!" Bear said. "Oh, how they bite!"

"Of course they bit you," Mole said, shaking his head. "Didn't you see the signs? They're everywhere. The field you were in is closed for construction. The ants are building a new anthill!"

"I didn't know!" said Bear. "I'm so sorry!"

Poor Bear! He made a mistake. Everyone makes mistakes sometimes. What do you do when you make a mistake?

Mole took Bear to see the new anthill.

It was truly amazing.

The ants were very hard workers. They climbed up tall ladders to put more sand and mud on their buildings.

Mole and Bear stayed all afternoon to watch. Other animals came, too.

"We never could have done so much work in so little time," they all agreed.

The next morning, the new anthill was done.

Mole and Bear sat on a hill nearby, admiring the ants' work.

Even when they weren't building, the ants were always busy. Some were bringing food to the anthill. Others watched out for enemies.

"They certainly know how to work, those ants," said Mole.

"We should teach them how to relax!" Bear added.

But the ants weren't interested. They loved to work.

"We'll relax for them," said Mole.

And so they did.

THE CAKE

In was Frog's birthday, and Auntie Mouse decided to bake him a cake. Auntie Mouse's cakes were famous.

For Frog, she made a cake with raisins and pine nuts. Anyone who passed Auntie Mouse's house while the cake was baking could smell how

good it was going to be.

When the cake was baked and cooled, Auntie Mouse put it in a basket and covered it with a cloth. Then she headed off to the pond. Frog lived nearby.

Have you ever helped to bake a cake? What's your favorite kind of cake?

On her way, she passed some birds. They sniffed and sniffed.

"What smells so good?" they asked her.

"I baked a cake for Frog's birthday," she told them. "I will bake one for you another time."

"Thank you!" said the birds.

On her way to Frog's house, Auntie Mouse stopped at the pond to see the new ducklings.

"They are so cute!" she told their parents.

"Thank you," said Mother Mallard.

Auntie Mouse couldn't resist. She put down her basket. Then she took a few crumbs of her cake and gave them to the ducklings.

But while her back was turned, a swan came up. He smelled the delicious cake. He didn't know it was for Frog, and he couldn't resist.

In two bites, he swallowed it all up!

"Oh, no!" cried Auntie Mouse when she saw what had happened. "What am I to do?"

Her friends the birds flew down to console her.

"We saw some beautiful raspberries nearby," they told her. "We can pick them and fill up your basket. Would that help?"

"Oh, thank you!" Auntie Mouse said.

The basket was soon full of berries. Auntie Mouse took it to Frog's house.

It wasn't a cake. But the raspberries were a big hit. And Frog had a very happy birthday!

THE SKATES

When Clover, the carpenter gnome, saw a picture of an ice skater, it gave him an idea.

He told his idea to Leveret the Rabbit. Leveret was the fastest roller-skater around.

"Your roller skates have four wheels that are lined up two by two," Clover said. "But if I could build them so that the wheels were lined up, just like ice skates, I could make a new kind of skate. It would go faster than any roller skates around."

Leveret thought this was a great idea. So Clover went to work.

Soon, Clover had built the new roller skates.

Leveret tried them. They were very fast and very smooth. Leveret loved them.

When the news spread about the new skates, everyone ran to Clover to get a pair.

Soon, everyone was skating. They wore special pads so they wouldn't get hurt if they fell.

Bear suggested a race.

Everyone was sure Bear would win, because he was so strong. Or perhaps the winner would be Leveret, since he had been skating longer than the others.

All the animals wore their safety pads. You always wear your safety equipment when you should, right? Why is this important?

But the surprise winner of the race was... Caterpillar! That was because he had the most legs.

The carpenter gnome had prepared a wonderful wooden cup for the winter.

Caterpillar was very proud!

THE BATTLE WITH A DRAGON

Little Squirrel's niece and nephew, Zip and Zap, had come for a sleepover.

Each time they came over, Little Squirrel would read to them before they went to sleep.

This time, she had found an old book on the dinosaurs that had lived on earth many years ago. The book also talked about dragons and other mythical creatures.

The two little squirrels fell asleep dreaming of these giants.

What do you think the dragons and dinosaurs did in Little Squirrel's story?

The next day, Little Squirrel was walking to the market when she met Lizard.

Lizard was usually very shy. He spent most of his time under a rock. But this morning he chatted awhile with Little Squirrel. Then he lay down to take a nap.

Lizard was awakened by someone shouting.

He opened his eyes.

There, in front of him, was a strange sort of cart.

On the cart were Zip and Zap Squirrel.

They had seen Lizard, and thought he was one of the dragons from Little Squirrel's book!

Zip had decided that they had to fight the fearsome creature right away.

Luckily, Beaver saw what was going on.

"Don't fight Lizard!" he called. "He may look a little different from you, but he is very nice. In fact, he's a friend of mine!"

Zip and Zap felt terrible. "We're sorry," they said. Then they explained about Little Squirrel's book.

"Some of my ancestors lived millions of years ago," said Lizard. "They probably knew some real dinosaurs."

"Wow!" said Zap.

"That's cool!" said Zip.

Later, Lizard helped Little Squirrel carry two heavy bags of potatoes home from the market.

"You're all invited to eat a big plate of fried potatoes at my house," she told Lizard, Zip, and Zap.

And that's just what everybody did.

THE SWIMMING POOL

Next to the pear tree there was a little spring. As time passed, it formed a small lake.

When the weather was hot, everyone went there for a swim. But the bottom of the lake was very muddy. Whenever folks swam there, they would climb out covered in mud.

Otter loved to swim, but she hated mud. So she got the idea to build a real swimming pool.

"We'll help!" said the busy Beaver family. They loved to work in the water.

The Beavers began by digging a big hole near the spring. Then they went to the river. There, they found little pebbles to put at the bottom of the pool.

Finally, they built a water wheel out of some sticks and some buckets. This wheel would help bring water from the spring to the new swimming pool.

Finally, the pool was done. Everyone came for a swim.

Of course, they were very careful. No one swam alone, and no one went near the pool if he didn't know how to swim. And Frog was always on guard to make sure the animals were safe.

Soon, the pool was the most popular place in the forest!

The Beavers were very proud of their work.

On the hottest days, one Beaver or another could always be found, proudly watching as the other animals swam.

Even the insects had fun in the pool.

"You and your family did a good job," Rabbit said to Mr. Beaver.

"Thank you," said Mr. Beaver.

From then on, each summer, all the animals swam at Beaver Pool.

THE QUAILS' NEST

One day, Auntie Mouse put on her best hat, took her umbrella, and set out to hear the singing contest. The Blackbirds had challenged the Nightingales to a competition. Everyone in the forest was going to be there.

"The Nightingales are sure to win," Auntie Mouse thought as she went on her way. "They have the most beautiful voices in the whole forest. But perhaps the Blackbirds have hatched a new bird who sings beautifully."

Auntie Mouse couldn't wait to find out. There was nothing nicer than hearing birds singing in the forest.

On the way, she ran into Mr. and Mrs. Quail. "Are you going to the concert?" she asked.

"I wish I could!" said Mrs. Quail. "But it's a chilly night, and I have to keep my eggs warm."

That's when Auntie Mouse had a wonderful idea.

She raced back home. There, she boiled some water. Then she filled up her hot water bag.

The bag was nice and warm. It would surely keep Mrs. Quail's eggs warm all night long!

She brought the bag back to the Quails.

"Your eggs will be warm and safe under my hot water bag," she told the two birds.

And so the Quails joined Auntie Mouse at the concert.

The Blackbirds sang beautifully. But as Auntie Mouse had predicted, the Nightingales won after all.

After the concert, Mr. and Mrs. Quail hurried home. They wanted to be sure their eggs were all right.

"Look!" laughed Auntie Mouse. "Look how well my hot water bag worked."

What a surprise! While the Quails had been listening to the singing, their eggs had hatched.

They were the parents of three new chicks!

"Chirp! Chirp! Chirp!" the three chicks cried.

The Quails were so grateful that they made Auntie Mouse the godmother of the chicks. And she was the best godmother ever!

TOM AND PENNY
AND THE GIANT EMERALD

Not far from the forest where
Robinson and his friends lived
was another special place. It
was the home of Tom and his
best friend, Penny.

Tom and Penny's forest was a magical place indeed, where flowers grew as high as trees. It was ringed by rows and rows of pine trees that kept the forest secluded.

And this was exactly how Tom and Penny liked it.

Tom's house was built in the stump of a big, old tree.

He loved waking up in his house. It was cozy and warm and full of things he had built himself.

Tom loved building things. He was very clever.

Every morning, he would get on his stationary bicycle. He had made the bicycle himself.

At the same time, he would read a book. Tom hated wasting time.

All this exercise was very good for him. It was also good for his friend, Penny.

The bicycle was hooked up to an electric generator that Tom had designed. It produced electricity for his house. It also supplied Penny's house with electricity. With this electricity, Penny powered everything in her house.

Look at all the things in Tom's house! Can you name some of them?

Penny lived nearby. Her house was surrounded by beautiful yellow daisies.

Penny loved flowers.

Near Penny's house, Tom had built a well so that she could have fresh water. She used the water to water her vegetable garden. Penny grew wonderful vegetables!

She also grew red geraniums in her window boxes.

The roof of Penny's house was made of a thick layer of hay. This was Tom's idea. Inside, the house was cooler in the summer and warmer in the winter.

Penny was a great gardener. She was also quite good at painting.

When she found out that Tom was learning to play baseball, she drew his portrait wearing his baseball cap and holding his bat.

"If you become a champion," said Penny, "everyone will want to have your portrait. That way, I will become famous, too!"

Tom was very proud of his portraits. He framed all of them and put them in his house.

WHAT HAPPENED TO PENNY

Penny was a good painter, and she was a good gardener.

She was also a good baker.

Penny could make the most delicious cakes in all the forest. She made wonderful cookies, too!

One day, Penny was busy baking. First, she made an apple pie. That was her specialty.

She also made a batch of almond cookies. They were for Tom.

She was so busy that she didn't hear the radio announcer.
"Attention!" he said. "Attila has been seen in the area.
Lock your doors and don't go out unless you have to!"

Attila was a big black rat. He was a terrible character. He had an emerald mine on the coast beyond the forest, and he loved his emeralds more than anything.

Attila would come to town to steal whatever he needed. He was also known to have taken some of the forest creatures back to his mine. There, he made them work like slaves.

When Squirrel heard the news about Attila, he was so frightened that he squeezed his toothpaste right out of the tube. Mouse spilled her tea, and Hedgehog stopped drying himself and almost fell down.

But Penny hadn't heard the news that day. And so she didn't know Attila had been seen nearby.

Penny had promised to bring Tom his cookies by nine o'clock that morning.

Unaware of the danger, she set out as usual.

She walked through the woods on the path to Tom's house, holding her basket.

She didn't know that Attila was watching her every move.

We know something will happen... and Penny does not know, does she? This gives the story "suspense." Can you think of other stories or movies that have suspense?

Suddenly, a net came out from nowhere.

In a flash, it had fallen over Penny, trapping her beneath.

"Why? What…? Who…? Help! Help!" yelled Penny.

The net had knocked her to the ground. The more she struggled to get free, the more she became entangled!

Penny looked up. There, standing over her, was the terrible black rat, Attila!

Penny was brave, but she knew what would happen to her. Attila would surely take her to his emerald mine and force her to work for him.

"Aha!" growled Attila. "What do we have here? A little white mouse with a basket of cookies! They smell good!"

"They're not for you!" Penny said bravely. "They're for my friend, Tom."

Attila just laughed. "I could use someone like you at my emerald mine," he said. "I need a cook! You're coming with me... and so are your cookies!"

TOM TO THE RESCUE

Attila put poor Penny in a cage behind his motorcycle. Then he sped away toward his emerald mine.

He passed through the desert on the way.

It was hot and dry inside the cage.

Penny hoped Tom would realize what had happened and come to save her.

In the meantime, Tom had been waiting for Penny for a long while.

He knew Penny was always on time.

He also knew that Attila had been spotted in the neighborhood.

So Tom decided to go to Penny's house.

Tom is brave, isn't he? When were some times when you have been brave?

Tom raced through the woods. When he got to Penny's house, he called and called. But no one answered. There was no trace of Penny.

The forest was very quiet. Everyone had probably stayed at home, afraid of Attila.

By now, Tom was worried. He began to walk along the path back to his house. He looked carefully at the ground the entire way, to see if he could find a trace of Penny.

Finally, he saw two marks in the road.

"These tracks were left by Attila's motorcycle!" Tom said to himself.

A short distance away in the leaves, he found the cloth that had covered the basket of cookies.

Now Tom was sure: Penny had been kidnapped by Attila!

"I will rescue her! That giant rat will not keep Penny for long!" Tom cried.

Tom walked quickly through the forest, following Attila's tracks. Soon, he reached the desert. It was very hot.

Suddenly, Tom saw a stranger sitting by a cactus. He was holding a red umbrella.

"Where are you going in this heat?" the stranger asked.

"And what are you doing here all by yourself?" asked Tom in return.

"My name is Leo. I travel here and there, repairing things for people," Leo explained.

"Did you see a big black rat pass this way?" Tom asked him.

"Yes, I did," said Leo.

"Well, the rat's name is Attila," Tom explained. "He has taken my friend Penny with him. I am following his tracks so I can set her free!"

"You'll need some help," Leo said. "It won't be easy to get across the desert... unless..."

"Unless what?" asked Tom.

"Unless we can build something that will get us across in a hurry!" said Leo.

"How and what can we build?" asked Tom.

Leo smiled. "Look!" he said. And from his bag, he pulled a strange tool.

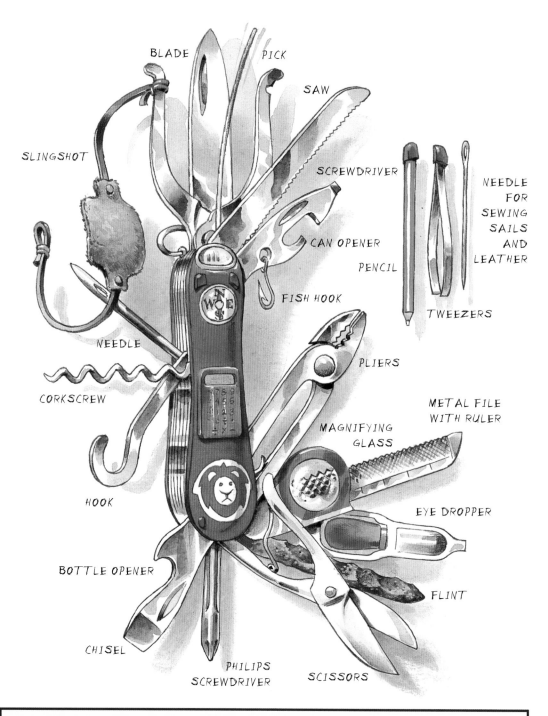

BLADE
PICK
SAW
SLINGSHOT
SCREWDRIVER
CAN OPENER
NEEDLE FOR SEWING SAILS AND LEATHER
PENCIL
FISH HOOK
TWEEZERS
NEEDLE
PLIERS
CORKSCREW
METAL FILE WITH RULER
MAGNIFYING GLASS
HOOK
EYE DROPPER
BOTTLE OPENER
FLINT
CHISEL
PHILIPS SCREWDRIVER
SCISSORS

Can you find the compass, light and calculator?

"This knife has gotten me out of many difficult situations," said Leo. "You'll see. It will help us this time, too!"

Tom had never seen anything like Leo's strange knife. It had everything a traveler might need. The first thing Tom and Leo did was to cut slices of cactus, which were left to dry in the sun. "These will be the wheels!" said Leo.

Then they collected some branches. Leo had some sturdy rope in his backpack. They used the rope to tie everything together.

Penny's cloth and the fabric
from Leo's umbrella made a
stout sail.

"But will it really work?"
asked Tom.

"Don't worry," said Leo.
"It will work. Now, we just
need a breeze!"

They waited and waited. Finally, the wind picked up…
and the strange cart started to move.

Soon, it was flying across the desert!

As the sun slowly went down, Tom saw a black speck in
the distance.

"Look!" he cried, pointing. "That's Attila's castle!"

"I told you we'd make it!" Leo smiled.

Tom and Leo made a cart out of scrap materials.
What could you use from your house to make a cart?

TERRIBLE ATTILA AND HIS HELPERS

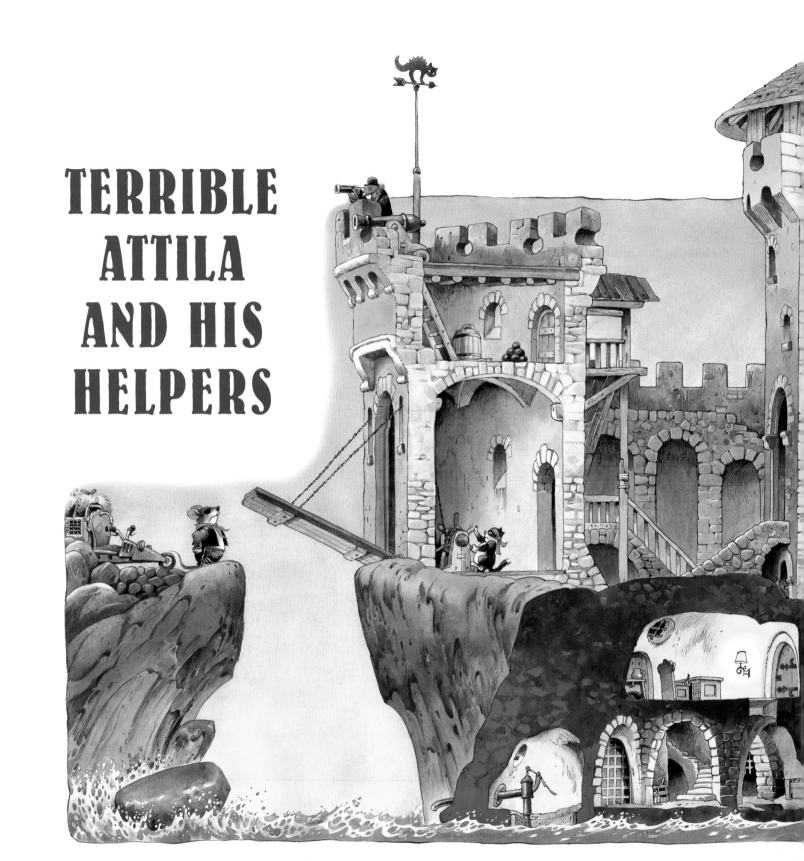

In the meantime, Attila and
his prisoner had
reached the castle.
"Let me in!"
Attila cried.
Bandit the cat
heard Attila
yelling and ran
to lower the
drawbridge.

BANDIT, The Cat

FALSAPERIA, The Weasel

Bandit the cat was one of Attila's helpers. The other two were a sneaky weasel named Falsaperia and a vulture named Bugsy.

"This is our new cook," Attila told them. "We will eat better from now on. And so will the prisoners... so they will be able to work even harder for us!"

BUGSY, The Vulture

Bandit, Falsaperia, and Bugsy were all evil creatures. But they all loved to eat... particularly Bugsy.

"Mmmm," they said. "You are wise, Attila, to bring a cook to feed us."

Poor Penny! Attila took her to the kitchen.

"Everything must be cleaned and put in order!" he told her. "You will prepare food for us and for the prisoners working in the mine. Remember that you are my prisoner. You must never disobey my orders!"

Penny, who had not said a word since she had been kidnapped, looked at the ugly black rat.

"I will not cook for anyone!" she said. "Not for you, and not for anyone else! If you do not set me free right this instant, you will be very sorry indeed!"

Attila laughed. "So," he said, sneering at her, "you don't want to work? Well, I'll show you!"

He locked Penny in an iron cage.

"No food or water for you," he told her. "I'll be back tomorrow. Maybe you'll change your mind."

Penny was furious. But she didn't say a word.

 Poor Penny must be scared. What could she do to be less frightened in her cage?

The next morning, Attila came back into the kitchen.

"So," he said to Penny, "do you want to come out of the cage, or do you want to stay in there?"

"I want to come out of the cage," Penny replied. "But I will only cook for the prisoners and not for you!"

Atilla laughed. "Maybe I should put you over the fire and warm you up a bit."

Penny knew that Attila was mean enough to do it. "All right," she said. "I'll cook for you, too."

Later, Bandit smelled something delicious coming from the kitchen.

"What are we eating today?" he asked, his mouth watering.

"When it's ready, you'll find out," Penny answered.

Bandit ate quickly. After he was done, he got to his feet.

"Now we have to take food to the prisoners," he told Penny. "Fill up a pot and come with me!"

When the weasel unlocked the room where the prisoners were kept, they all ran to greet Penny.

They had known her in the forest, before they were captured by Attila.

The Hedgehog had been the first to be captured. His job was to dig the emeralds from the walls of the mine.

The Frog had been captured next. He had to load the jewels onto the cart.

The Tortoise separated the stones from the dirt. He washed them in a special sieve.

The Mouse made the last check, to make sure none of the emeralds were missed.

And the Dormouse worked the pump that pumped the dirty water out to sea again.

Attila himself examined all the stones after they were cleaned. He looked at the stones one by one and threw away those that were scratched or imperfect.

He kept only the very best stones. He cut them with a large grindstone. And when they were shined and polished, he placed them in his enormous collection.

Attila loved his emeralds. Sometimes, in the middle of the night, he would dream that someone had stolen them. He would wake up in fear.

Then he would go downstairs and count them all to make sure that none were missing.

"One day, I'll be the richest rat in the world!" he would mumble to himself as he fell asleep.

TOM AND LEO ARRIVE

Tom and Leo arrived at the castle in the middle of the night.

"How are we going to get in?" Tom wondered. The walls of the castle were very high.

"We'll just tie some rocks to this rope and throw it over the weathervane," Leo said confidently. Then we'll climb across!"

Of course, it was easier said than done. But finally, Leo got the rope in the right position.

Then they started to climb across to the castle.

The black cat on the weathervane seemed to be watching them. It made Tom a little nervous. But Tom knew it was just his imagination.

Tom tried not to look down as they climbed the rope.

But he couldn't help himself.

The water looked dark and cold.

Luckily, they soon were across.

Leo turned on his flashlight. The little tool was sure coming in handy!

The two of them crept down the steps of the castle.

Soon, they came to a door.

They didn't notice the yellow eyes behind them…

They crept toward the door and quietly opened it.

Inside, they could see Attila, sitting at his giant desk. At his side were the weasel Falsaperia and Nero, the vulture.

"What do we do now?" whispered Tom.

 Whose eyes do you think they are?
How did the follower find Tom and Leo?

But there wasn't time to do anything before they were pushed into the room.

"I've been expecting you!" said Attila. Chuckling with satisfaction, he pushed a lever—and a trap door opened in the floor beneath Tom and Leo!

"Two more slaves for my emerald mine!" Attila said as they fell. "Welcome to my castle!"

TOM'S PLAN

Leo and Tom hit the ground with a thud. They found themselves in a small cell behind bars.

Then Tom saw his old friends: the Hedgehog, the Tortoise, the Frog, the Mouse, and the Dormouse. "Where did you come from?" they all cried.

Tom was just about to tell them when he heard a noise.

"Dinner time!" called Bandit the cat. In front of him, carrying a pot of food, was Penny!

When she saw Tom, she gasped. "How did you get here?" she whispered.

"I came to rescue you," he told her.

Bandit cracked his whip. "No talking!" he shouted. "Back to the kitchen with you! And the rest of you, back to work!"

Tom and Leo had to work in the mine, too, in order to earn their small bowls of soup.

"Don't move the pile of stones in the corner!" the Frog warned.

"Why not?" Leo asked.

"It's a secret," the Frog whispered. "We found an emerald so big that no one could ever believe it! But we don't want to give it to Attila."

"Oh, my! May we see it?" asked Tom.

The Frog carefully moved the stones. It was the biggest emerald Tom and Leo had ever seen.

They covered the green gem back up with sand and rocks.

That night, the animals talked of escaping from their prison.

"We've tried many times," said the Dormouse. "But none of our plans have worked."

"We'll figure out a way," Tom said.

And they soon did.

"We can use the emerald as bait," Tom said. "Attila would do anything for an emerald of that size!

"We'll leave a note in the cooking pot that Penny leaves here," he went on. "Bandit is sure to find it and give it to Attila.

"When Attila comes here to get the emerald, we will refuse to give it to him. He will have to follow us into the mine.

"Then we'll find a way to open the sluice gate," Tom went on. "The sea water will rush in. Attila and his gang will be overcome by the water. And we will be able to escape."

"It's a good plan," Leo said. "Let's hope it works!"

The next day, everything went as planned. Attila came down to the dungeon with his scheming helpers.

"Give me that emerald!" shouted Attila. "It belongs to me. You found it in my mine!"

"We will give it to you if you set us free!" said Tom.

"Show me the stone," Attila demanded.

Tom showed Attila the emerald. Attila looked at it greedily.

"Give it to me!" he shouted. "I order you to give it to me!"

"Run!" Tom shouted to his friends. They all ran toward the tunnel, following Tom's plan.

Attila ordered his helpers to raise the metal gate of the prison.

"Hurry!" he shouted. "Don't let them get away!"

THE INSIDE OF THE MINE

The emeralds were washed with water from the sluice gate (7). It was never opened all the way, because it led to the sea. Tom's plan was to open this gate.

1. trap door
2. pump, to pump water from the bottom of the well
3. pipe to drain water into sea
4. well
5. water- and air-tight door
6. tunnel
7. sluice-gate
8. weight
9. counter weight
10. winch
11. candle

THE END OF ATTILA

Attila and his three followers raced after the prisoners. Soon, they reached the area where the stones were washed.

There, they found the emerald, which Tom had left in plain sight.

The big rat grabbed the emerald. He held it carefully. He knew that if he dropped it, it could break into a thousand pieces.

But while Attila and his evil helpers stared at the emerald, a candle flame was burning under the rope that held the sluice gate closed. Tom had left the candle there.

With a snap, the rope broke. The gate went up. And the room filled with water!

Attila and his helpers were carried away in a rush of water. Attila couldn't even hold onto the emerald. It was torn out of his hand in the water.

In the meantime, Tom and his friends waited at the end of the tunnel. They were sitting in a barrel. And when the water level rose, they rose up with it.

As they floated to the top of the tunnel, Tom saw something green and sparkling in the water.

He reached out and grabbed it.

When they reached the top, only an iron door stood between them and their freedom.

But it was locked!

What do you think Tom found? Have you ever found something exciting?

In the meantime, Penny had heard their shouts. She was waiting on the other side of the locked gate.

Leo took his special knife out and began trying each tool.

The screwdriver didn't work. The saw was too small. Finally, he tried a small steel pick.

The lock clicked open. They were free!

"Hooray for Leo!" they all shouted.

They ran out of the castle and across the drawbridge—just as they heard the footsteps of someone behind them!

"Attila must have gotten through an escape door in the mine!" gasped Tom.

"No worries," said Leo. "Here's Attila's motorcycle and cart!"

"We won't fit!" said the Mouse.

"We'll just have to squeeze in," said Tom. "Hang on, everyone!"

The bike took off, and Tom and his friends headed back to their forest home.

HOME AGAIN!

When Tom and Penny and the others arrived home on the bike, everyone was thrilled to see them.

"We'll have a feast!" they all said. "We'll celebrate your homecoming!"

Everyone looked curiously at Leo. Then Tom introduced him and explained how Leo had helped him free Penny and the others.

"Hooray for Leo!" everyone shouted.

Leo felt very much at home. And he decided to stay in the forest forever.

Tom gave him the giant emerald as a souvenir.

Leo never sold it. He kept it as a reminder of his great adventure with Tom and Penny!

What special objects have you kept to remind you of an important event or adventure?